FIVE LITTLE KITTY CATS

Story By May Purnell • Pictures by Dorothy Purnell

LAUGHING ELEPHANT • MMXV

FIVE LITTLE
KITTY CATS

There were once five happy, fluffy, little Kitty Cats. They were as different as five merry little Kitty Cats could be. One was gray. One was snow white. One was yellow as gold. One had lovely stripes and one—now would you believe it—was PINK.

KITTY CATS

They lived in a little house on a riverbank. There was a porch with white pillars. Roses climbed all over the porch. Sometimes little birds made their nests among the roses. These five little Kitty Cats loved birds and were very kind to them.

And out in the yard grew a great cat-al-pa tree. The branches were very smooth.
They made fine slides. When the five little Kitty Cats slid down they went so fast it was
almost like flying right through the air—as though they had WINGS!

KITTY CATS

Upstairs five little beds stood in a row, and each had a ribbon the color of the Kitty Cat sleeping there. Except the gray Kitty Cat's. THAT was red. Early in the morning, when the sun peeped in the window, up jumped the Kitty Cats and washed their faces.

They had their breakfast, and washed the dishes and put them away. They were very careful not to break any. Striped Kitty Cat and Yellow Kitty Cat swept the floor. Then they all went out to work in the garden.

But White Kitty Cat did not work in the garden. She stayed home to make cap-nip cookies for tea. There were pussy-willows in the garden. And under the cat-al-pa tree were rows of cat's-foot, chickweed, mouse-ear, and other plants that Kitty Cats love.

FIVE LITTLE
KITTY CATS

Some busy little bees had built a home in a beehive in the garden. Somebody's hoe upset the beehive. THAT upset the five little Kitty Cats, too–Oh, very much. Such a scrambling and running and scampering you never saw.

FIVE LITTLE
KITTY CATS

Into the house rushed all the Kitty Cats, with loud wailings. The angry little bees had nipped every one. White Kitty Cat bandaged all the stings. Soon they felt very much better and were ready for catnip mousse. Next day the Kitty Cats were well again.

FIVE LITTLE
KITTY CATS

They all went fishing. Gray Kitty Cat hooked a fine red mullet. White Kitty Cat caught a silver fish. Yellow Kitty Cat angled for a gold fish. Striped Kitty Cat hunted along the bank for turtles, and Pink Kitty Cat cast a net for shrimp.

FIVE LITTLE
KITTY CATS

Then Striped Kitty Cat fell off the rocks right into the river. Splash! The little fish swam away as fast as they could go. All the other Kitty Cats pulled striped Kitty Cat into the boat. Such a wet Kitty Cat you never saw!

Every Sunday the Kitty Cats went along the wooded path to church. Each carried a parasol with a big bow on top the color of its fur. Except Gray Kitty Cat. HERS was red.

KITTY CATS

Sometimes in the summer they had picnics under the cat-al-pa tree. They had lovely things to eat. Catnip jam and mouse-ear sandwiches. All the Kitty Cats wore ribbons to match their fur. Except Gray Kitty Cat. HERS was red.

But when it was cold, at twilight, the Kitty Cats sat at their little table in front of the fire to eat their supper. What do you think the Kitty Cats ate for their supper? They are bread and milk in lovely blue bowls. Then they went happily to bed.

KITTY CATS

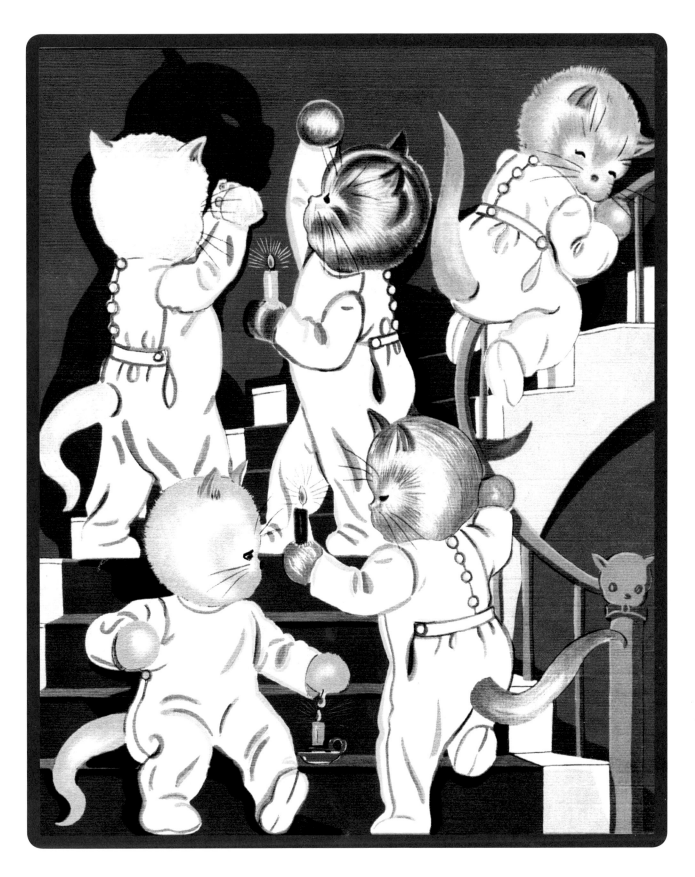

Each Kitty Cat carried a candle. Sometimes they made shadow pictures on the walls with their paws. Sometimes they slid down the bannister. Wouldn't it be fun to go along that quiet woodland path to the cottage of the Kitty Cats on the riverbank?

COPYRIGHT © 2015, BLUE LANTERN STUDIO

ISBN/EAN: 9781595839398

THIS PRODUCT CONFORMS TO CPSIA 2008
FIRST PRINTING • PRINTED IN CHINA THROUGH COLORCRAFT LTD, HONG KONG • ALL RIGHTS RESERVED
THIS IS A REPRINT OF A BOOK FIRST PUBLISHED IN 1940.

LAUGHING ELEPHANT
3645 INTERLAKE AVENUE NORTH SEATTLE, WA 98103

LAUGHINGELEPHANT.com